CATTYWAMPUS

ROBERT FORD AND JOHN BODEN

CATTYWAMPUS

© 2019 by Robert Ford and John Boden

Cover art © 2019 by whutta.com

ACKNOWLEDGEMENTS

For Frank Errington, a soul of depthless kindness and support.

For Andy Pete, a fellow dreamer and sometimes sillyheart. Rest well, brother.

Thank you to friends and family—new or old, here or not. We wear you in our hearts and during all we do.

*Ah! Well a-day! What evil looks had I
from old and young!*

The Rime of the Ancient Mariner
— Samuel Taylor

CHAPTER 1
TUESDAY AROUND DUSK

"What in the Sam Hill are you doing with that?" Darlene reached out to grab Sheila's forearms and eased them downward. "And you know there are video cameras in the damned store, dontcha?"

Sheila grinned at her and gave a snorting laugh. "And *you* know the damned things haven't worked in over eight months, *dontcha?*" That last word spat out in a sneer more than a joking manner. "And the outside ones ain't worked in years!" Sheila walked around the counter, stood facing the cash register, and then jerked her hands upward, aiming a small silver pistol toward the wood paneled wall behind. Drawing a bead on the EMPLOYEES MUST WASH THEIR HANDS sign hanging there. "Gimme all your money, bitch!"

Darlene made a face and shook her head. "Gonna fuck around and shoot a tit off."

"Doubt it." The woman put her hands down and twisted her hips back and forth so her large breasts jiggled. "These things are bullet proof. Hell, they're so big I could lose one, part the one left down the middle, and still have a bigger pair than most of the ginches in this town."

Darlene nodded at the gun. "Hell'd you get that thing, anyway?"

"Jakey came home piss drunk last night. Again. Passed out on the shitter and I didn't find him until this morning when I heard him fall over against the bathtub. Damn jeans were soaked with pee and stinking. Puke in the toilet." Sheila put the pistol back in her purse, tucked away beneath the counter.

"He's an asshole."

"Oh, I know he is, but look at me, honey." She put her hands on her hips. "This late in life, my *only* choices are assholes. You, now…" Sheila stepped toward the food counter and pulled on a pair of clear disposable gloves. "Young, beautiful thing like you? Got your whole life ahead of you, honey. Oh hell, to go back thirty years and be sixteen again? Oh, shit would be different, I tell you."

"I guess so. I still think you could do better than Jakey." Darlene walked away from the register to turn off the coffee pots. "*I* think you're pretty."

"That's awful sweet of you to say, hon." Sheila smiled at the girl and lowered her voice to a whisper, even though the Gas 'n Go was empty except for the two of them. "The pistol's not the only thing I swiped from Jakey." Her smile grew to a grin. She reached into her purse and held up a small baggie of pot pinched between two fingers.

Darlene laughed out loud and then tried to hide her reaction as a beat-up Dodge truck pulled up to the pumps outside. She had seen the pick-up and its driver before. He'd been a regular the last several weeks, usually stopping by in the late evening for a fill up or some smokes. A young guy, but old enough to buy beer. You could tell he worked in construction or maybe as a roofer, wiry and lean. He usually wore concert t-shirts with the sleeves cut off, from bands she'd never heard of. Darlene had to admit, she took notice he had a hell of a tan. *Mr. Tan* was the nickname they referred to him by when he wasn't around.

Darlene pulled the used coffee filters from the coffee makers and tossed them into the garbage, but she took her time, glancing out at him as he stepped from the Dodge and stood beside it with a cigarette.

He had the look of someone who hadn't been smoking very long and was doing it to try and look cool. He took another drag and flicked it—*cool*—into the patch of muddy grass to the right of the building.

Darlene focused on the last of the coffee filters as he walked into the store. He glanced at her with a nod and a slight smile and headed toward the beer coolers in the rear.

Flicking the power switch on the last coffee maker, Darlene walked straight toward the cash register. She caught Sheila's eyes as she stepped behind the counter and noticed the woman held one of the Gas 'n Go's *BIG EIGHT INCHER* hot dogs in her gloved hand. Sheila tilted her head and rolled her eyes back in her head as she twirled the hot dog and thrust her hips along with it.

Darlene's face flushed. She bit her lip and turned away from the woman. *Sheila was on fire tonight. God, did she take a puff of weed before she got here? Then again, Sheila hadn't been her normal self since Saturday night.*

Mr. Tan carried a six-pack of Miller and a bag of Funyuns to the counter, and then grabbed two ready-made chilidogs from beneath the heat lamp. He set them beside the beer and flashed a smile. "Pack of Marlboro Reds, too, please."

He reached for his wallet as Darlene grabbed a pack of cigarettes and rang up the items. "Looks like a bachelor kind of evening."

"Doesn't have to be."

He smiled as he spoke, and Darlene smiled back automatically, feeling heat rise in her cheeks. His hand brushed hers as he handed cash over. His fingertips surprisingly smooth and soft.

"Four dollars and sixty-eight cents is your..." Her words caught as her throat dried up.

"Change?" Mr. Tan's smile widened to a grin as he held his hand out for his money. Darlene counted out the last few coins one by one into his palm. The last coin was a quarter and the metallic clink sounded off, different somehow than it should.

The front door to the Gas 'n Go swung wide open in a hard rush.

The guy came in with his head down and his hands jammed into the pockets of the ratty-ass hoodie he wore, a brazen *fuck you!* to the temps outside fluttering close to ninety degrees. He looked up at the ladies behind the counter and the skinny fella, as he walked quickly to the back corner by the Freezee dispenser. In a motion so swift no one actually saw it, he jumped and swung his hand and the sound of cracking plastic and breaking glass followed. Darlene glanced up at the remnants of the broken camera, dangling like a large rat with its tail in a trap. "Hey!"

"Shut it." The man was right behind Mr. Tan, with his hands back in his pockets but one of them thrust forward and upwards to amplify the something he had aimed at them. "And don't fucking move. I'm nervous as hell and this thing has a hair trigger." He tried to smile but it was just a limp crooked thing. His sweatshirt had ridden up to expose his midriff, and Darlene noticed the lacework of scars covering it.

"I want all the money. As in every *fucking* penny. The register. The fucking Cancer Can, all of it." With that, he stepped forward and poked Mr. Tan with the gun in his pocket. "You can add your fortune to the pile as well, Pumpkin."

The tanned man smiled. "Well, being as we've taken big steps past fucking formalities, why don't ya just call me Billy?"

Mr. Tan took a swing.

The man in the hoodie's expression became a mask of absolute terror.

There was a loud sound like someone dropping a brick in a steel drum.

Billy fell to the floor, slow as molasses, with half of his head missing.

Time stopped.

CHAPTER TWO

"Oh God." Darlene cupped her hand to her mouth and stared at the cute, tanned construction worker's corpse on the dirty linoleum. A lagoon of bright red around his head. "Sheila, what... what did you..."

"I didn't... I didn't mean to!" Sheila held the pistol straight in front of her with shaking hands, pointing toward the man in the hoodie. Her face was bleached of color, like an oil rag left out in the summer sun for months.

"Jesus fucking Christ, lady!" Mr. Hoodie sidestepped the rapidly growing puddle of blood at his feet. "What'd ya do that for?"

Darlene's cupped hand fell from her face. "She was trying to shoot *you*, asshole!"

He spun to face Darlene and his hoodie pulled back to reveal more of his face—pimpled with sparse patches of hair, framed with greasy brown curls.

Sheila's mouth opened in realization and she whispered out loud. "You're a fuckin' kid. Sweet weepin' Christ, just a kid." Her hands were shaking and she lowered them down to the counter.

"Who was trying to *rob* us!" Darlene grabbed a handful of beef sticks from the container on the counter and threw them at the kid. "Asshole!" She followed that up by flinging steel cigarette lighter cases. One of the cases with a picture of a bass on it caught him above his left eye. He yelped and brought both hands up in defense.

Darlene froze in place, a handful of steel lighter cases in her grip. Her gaze was focused on Mr. Hoodie. "Is *that*..." She cocked her head, staring. "Are you kidding me?"

Sheila still had a whitewash complexion and looked ready to vomit, but at Darlene's words, she turned to the kid and looked him over. A light bulb went off. Gripped in the kid's right hand was a stainless-steel garden hose nozzle. She could see the handle was wrapped in duck tape.

A pretend gun. For a pretend robber.

"You *stupid* motherfucker!" Sheila spit her words in disgust. "That's not even a real gun!"

The kid raised his hands in surrender and opened them to show empty palms, allowing the fake pistol to drop to the floor with a thin metal clank. His hood fell back from his face completely, revealing red-rimmed eyes and a runny nose appearing to have been wiped with sandpaper the last few days. "You don't understand. It's not what you think. It's not—"

"Fuckin' meth head!" Sheila raised the pistol with trembling hands, and leveled it at the kid's face.

His expression as he watched wasn't one of fear for his own life, but something else entirely. He blinked slowly at Sheila and shook his head ever so slightly. "I wouldn't do that if I were you."

"Why the hell not? Gimme *one* reason I oughtn't give you an extra mouth in your forehead and call the cops?" Sheila's voice was shrill and grating. It was the tone that pissed Jakey off so much when they argued. She saw Darlene wince at the sound but didn't care.

Darlene looked at the young man, soaking in his own skin, and a look of sympathy to wash over her Avon-abused face. "What are you doing? You look all of sixteen, and here you are, tearing your life off at the dotted line for *what?* Maybe fifty-seven dollars and change?"

Darlene stepped away from the counter and cradled her stomach. Her tone was the same Sheila had heard her use with her little brother, Chester, when he needed to calm down.

"I need the money." Abruptly, the kid's voice leapt from him, his eyes widening in surprise as if he wasn't even aware he could speak. "I gotta get the fuck outta this shitstain town."

Sheila followed the kid's quick glance at the door—all it offered was a view of the empty lot and Mr. Tan's truck still parked at the pumps. There were no flashing lights, no bullhorn blaring. *God bless a flyspeck town where a gunshot at sunset doesn't cause a panic.*

The boy found a smile within and made his mouth work to wear it.

"I swear on all that is holy, I didn't want to hurt no one." He looked down at the man on the floor, the halo of dark red surrounding his head. "Honest." The last word came out a whisper. He raked a shaking hand up through greasy hair splayed up like wild grass. "I really fucked it this time."

He started to pace, his hands opening and closing like hatchling's mouths, and Darlene put her hands over her stomach, her expression distraught. Sheila figured the kid reminded Darlene of her brother, but there was no room here for bleedin' hearts. The fuckin' kid had tried to rob the place!

Sheila, gripped the gun in her hand, and licked her lips. She drew back a dollop of chili on the corner of her mouth, and felt an odd smile began to grow.

CHAPTER THREE
THE PREVIOUS SATURDAY NIGHT AROUND 8PM

"You thieving cow, I'm paying you to sell them wieners, not neck 'em!"

Mr. Blevins was hollering again. Always. Sheila stood still and tried to pretend he hadn't caught her eating chilidogs again.

"I know you fucking hear me!" The man stepped closer to her, his crooked nose and stinking breath inches from her face. "You're done this time, Missy. Go get your purse and your sweatshirt. And go steal the snatch corks from the bathroom and whatever else you think you can get and get the fuck outta here."

"I'm sorry, Mr. Blevins! I didn't get a chance to eat before—"

"Fired, it's called. Shitcanned by the less eloquent. And it ain't up for debate or reconsideration. You've had more chances than I can count. Get gone, girlie." With that, the old man turned and stepped to the register. A young woman stood there looking embarrassed for witnessing the display. Blevins screwed on his official false face and grinned at the customer.

"That it, Ma'am?" He asked, smiling wide and pouring enough sugar over the words to kill a diabetic. He scanned her jug of milk and paused before putting the scanner gun down.

"Yeah, that's it." The woman stole a quick look at the crying girl in the back room, the one stuffing her sweatshirt into her bag and wiping her eyes on her arm.

Sheila stomped out past the both of them and through the front of the store, the cowbell on the door clanging as she fled.

"Three bucks even." Mr. Blevins winked and the lady handed him a five. He gave her the change, wished her a wonderful night, and watched her leave the store.

The large man who was at the coolers approached the counter. He sat down a jug of iced tea and nodded towards the smokes behind the counter. He was a regular and Blevins grabbed two packs of Marlboro reds without so much as asking.

"On a run, Deke?" He asked, punching register buttons with a calloused fingertip.

"Seems like I always am." The man replied without meeting Blevins' gaze. He smoothed the ragged beard on his chin and grabbed the cigarettes from the counter. He made them disappear into his flannel pocket quicker than any magician could. "It ain't a long run so I can get back and see the wife a bit before the next one."

"Give my best to Lucille. And safe travels to you."

Deke pocketed his change and nodded as he turned and exited the door.

Blevins turned the corner to go through to the office. The milk lady and Deke had barely left the parking lot before Blevins started screaming to an empty store. "That cunt shit in the fuckin' sink!"

Chapter Four

"You're gonna do whatever the fuck we say you do." Sheila's voice had lost its tremor, instead evening out to a flatline calm. "Comin' in here with a fake gun. Jumped up Jesus Christ in a sidecar... the shitmess you done tracked in here!"

Sheila wore a squirrely smile, slanted sideways and off kilter.

Darlene felt a shiver run through her at the sight. It scared her, and the worst part of it was she wasn't exactly sure why.

"Dance." Sheila punctuated it by raising the gun and pointing it into the kid's face.

The boy glanced at Darlene and then back to Sheila. "What?"

"Dance, fucker. Let me see your moves." She steadied the pistol further out in front of her.

"I don't... *what?*"

Sheila pulled the trigger and the glass door in front of the Red Bull detonated. One of the cans spewed amber liquid out onto the floor. The boy's arms flew up to his side as he winced.

"Goddamn it, Sheila!" Darlene's ears rang from the shot and Sheila never even turned to look at her.

"Fuckin' *dance*. I wanna see moves like Jagger, boy." Sheila's smile thinned out and her eyes darkened.

The boy let out a shaky breath and started swinging his hips and moving his arms to a song that only played in his head.

"Looks like some 80's *Breakfast Club* shit. Get better. Get *into* it for Chrisssakes!" Sheila giggled at herself.

Darlene stared at Sheila and it was obvious *she* was *into it*. Darlene knew the look. It was like her mom's boyfriend, Darnell, stinking of liquor and staggering through the trailer. It was like her brother, Chester, when he stared off into the Great Nothing and mumbled to himself.

This wasn't good. Sheila's cheese had slid off her cracker. Darlene chewed her bottom lip and tried to figure out a way to wrangle this.

The boy moved to the rack of potato chips and started moonwalking or whatever the palsied shuffle foot thing he was doing was called, as he stared at Sheila for some kind of approval. His worn sneakers moved through the edge of Mr. Tan's blood puddle and he slid, unexpectedly, too far. The boy's expression changed to immediate fear, as if his performance had miserably failed and he was waiting for the crowd to boo. From Michael Jackson to Urkel in the blink of an eye.

"All right, okay. Enough. Fuckin' hell."

"Sheila?" Darlene almost whispered the word, but the woman didn't turn her way. "Sheila?" A little louder this time.

"What?"

"What's next? What're you… what're *we* gonna do?"

Sheila hugged the pistol close to her chest, the barrel still pointed at the boy as she glared at him. The harsh fluorescent light sharpened the beads of sweat on the boy's face and the spatters of blood on his skin.

"I'm gettin' bored with him. Let's put him in back."

"With Mr—"

Sheila snapped her focus on Darlene. "Why the fuck not?"

Darlene opened her mouth to say something and then shut it. Sheila's gaze was a razor blade.

Waving the gun in front of her, Sheila moved from behind the counter. "Move along, dipshit. Toward the coolers in the back. Keep your damned grubby hands where I can see 'em."

The boy held his hands up and scuffed toward the rear of the store, pausing at the fizzing puddle of Red Bull and a tall silver door with a heavy handle.

"Toby." He sighed heavily through his nose. "My name so's ya can stop with the boy shit."

"Open the door up, moron."

He popped the latch on the door and a thick flow of iced air rushed free.

Darlene's hands felt sweaty against the dirty counter. "Sheila—"

"What?" Her voice had an edge to it that hadn't been there all evening. Before, it had held a tone of amusement, *joy* almost, but now it was pissy and full of briars.

Darlene shook her head. "Nothin."

"Get in, kid." A pause. "Oh, I'm sorry. Where are my manners... get in, *Toby*." She amplified her snark with a big smile that looked like it was carved from rusted tin.

"I'll fuckin' freeze to death!" His expression was pained, way over his head in a shitshow he never intended on being part of. He let go of the door and it slowly closed.

"Maybe you will, maybe you won't. But if you don't step inside that fuckin' cooler, I'll open your head up like a can of Spam and you can die on the floor like Mr. GQ smooth over by the counter." She cocked the hammer on the pistol and the clicking sound was very loud in the store. "Your call."

Toby flipped the hood of his sweatshirt up over his head and yanked the chewed drawstrings to tighten it around his face. He glanced at Darlene she saw the expression of fear and regret on his face.

She looked away as Sheila poked him in the chest with the gun. "You waiting for a fucking invitation?"

Toby reached out and swung the door open again.

"In." Sheila kicked him hard in the ass and he stumbled into the cooler. She reached forward and pushed the door shut, quickly sliding the pin through the bolt before he could start pounding and get it open. Sheila stood with her forehead against the cold metal, and Darlene saw her lick the gun's barrel with the tip of her tongue and closed her eyes.

Yeah, Darlene thought, this train is on a whole different track.

The yelling from inside the cooler was muffled by the thick walls and the hum of the fans. But there was definitely yelling.

CHAPTER FIVE

Toby sat on the frigid concrete, hugging his knees. His throat hurt from screaming to be let out and he had finally given up. He pulled a tarnished Zippo lighter from his jeans and lit up a flickering pocket of light. He crab-walked to the door and kicked it with all he had. It didn't budge.

"You're fucked." He whispered to himself and watched the words float around him in a puff of breath. He took a minute to survey the setting. Toby scanned the back wall and noted several plastic soda crates, as well as a few cardboard flats that once housed beer. There was a roll of paper towels lying beside a frosted puddle of red. Near that rested a broom and a plastic bucket. The bucket was dotted with more red spots. Toby stepped forward and peered into the plastic basin.

It was half full of teeth. *Bloody* teeth. As in these didn't just *fall the fuck out of someone's mouth* kinda teeth. He cringed and turned to run—where to, he had no idea—and then he saw the body in the corner.

"Christ on a cracker!" He hollered as he recognized Boscoe T. Blevins, a miserable fuck of a man, and owner of the squalid Gas 'n Go. He was slumped to the side and there wa a thick rope of black dangling from his bottom lip. His tongue hung from the corner of his mouth like a slug. His eyes were open and the left one bulged from the socket, the section of forehead above it dark purple and swollen. The right side of his face was in no better shape. The ear there looked like it was made of clay and had been molded by a five-year old.

Toby hunkered down and looked the dead man in his glassy eyes. "What the hell happened to you?" He glanced at the bucket of teeth, leaned backward and slipped on a frozen patch on the cooler floor. Toby's right foot kicked out and hit the bucket, making a despicable rustling noise as the teeth slid against one another before it spilled over in a scatter of white marbles. Toby paled and his mouth opened to let out a scream, but no sound followed through.

It wasn't the spilled teeth—not entirely.

It was the two small hands, not-so-neatly severed at the wrists, which lay upon the teeth like the main course of some grisly feast.

It was the sparkly pink nail polish on the little nails at the tips of the little fingers.

After a few feeble attempts, Toby was able to scream.

And scream some more.

CHAPTER SIX

"He's freakin' out in there."

"Asshole should've thought about it before he tried to rob the place." Sheila set the pistol on the counter. "Fuckin' dumbass. If it hadn't been for him, we'd be the goddamn town heroes tonight."

Darlene heard heavy thumps as the kid beat against the inside of the cooler. The pin on the latch rattled but held. His already muffled screams stopped. She turned to Sheila again. "So, what now? If we… if you let him live, then we'll get—"

"I don't know yet!" Sheila took a deep breath and let it out slow as she chewed on her lower lip. "Haven't decided. That son of a bitch, Blevins…"

"And you really… I mean, look Sheila… we've known each other a while now, and I trust you, okay? But you *really* found that stuff in Blevins's truck?"

Sheila glanced at her with a look of disgust and then barked a reply. "Well I didn't stop by the fuckin' elementary school and pick them up myself, for Chrissakes!"

"Sorry." Darlene's apology was quiet. This wasn't how tonight was supposed to go down. Not at all. It was supposed to be neat and clean and easy. A fake robbery and then Sheila was supposed to pop her a good one in the mouth for healthy measure to make it believable when the cops showed up.

But then Sheila had to go and get fired. And that meant Blevins was eagle-eying every goddamn thing and came to the store because he didn't

ROBERT FORD AND JOHN BODEN

think Darlene was competent enough to handle an overnight on her own.

Why in the hell Sheila didn't just up and leave when she got here and saw Blevins's truck is beyond me.

Darlene avoided looking directly at Sheila for fear of being yelled at again.

But no, she had pulled her car off to the edge of the parking lot and then stuck her nose in Blevins's truck, probably looking for things to steal or maybe to pour a can of cola in his gas tank.

When Sheila brought the bucket into the shop, she had her purse strap across her body and was holding the tire iron at her side. The look on Blevins's face as he first recognized Sheila, and then registered the bucket of teeth was like watching summer roadkill decompose in fast forward. Darlene had never known you could *hear* a person sweat but damned if she didn't convince herself she heard a low-grade hiss as his pores pissed themselves.

After that, things happened fast.

CHAPTER SEVEN
SUNDAY NEARING MIDNIGHT

"Sheila! I thought I..." His words were amputated when she shoved the end of the jack handle into his face hard enough to break his front tooth in half.

"Not another fucking word. Not a sound. And don't you move, you fucking sicko!" Sheila's face seemed to stretch to accommodate the force of the words she bellowed at him.

Darlene stood by the register, nervous and not at all sure what was happening. "Sheila?" she managed before the other woman sneered at her.

"I saw Fucko's truck outside and had every intention of stealing whatever I could from it. Hoped he had tools or something in there I could ruin for him. I opened the truck and meant to shit in it and saw this bucket on the floor in the passenger side." The longer she went on, the less loud she got, her voice evaporating and getting brittle. Her eyes were brimming with wet and she never once took her gaze off Blevins.

"What is it? What's in the bucket?" Darlene felt her mouth smiling against her will, she stepped away from the register and closer to the doorway. Sheila sat the bucket loudly on the floor, the sound from within like M&Ms being shaken in a can. Darlene leaned and looked and the befuddlement devouring her face was absolute. There was a stretching taffy minute before her mouth started to work soundlessly like a gasping fish. She wheeled around and looked the older man in the eyes. "The fuck! Are those teeth?"

Blevins said nothing. His tongue crept out cautiously to remove the blood trickling from his lip. He cleared his throat and began to speak. "I can explain... I mean it ain't exactly what it—" And then a bad thing happened. Blevins's lips began to form a smile.

The sound of the tire iron against the man's forehead was a giant stomping the silence of a village. Blevins's mouth kept moving, his damaged brain trying to stitch lies, as Sheila swung again and again. By the time she stopped, bits of it were all over the counter behind him, as well as all over Darlene's tits.

He pointed to the bucket and coughed a bubble of blood that gift-wrapped the last words he'd ever utter. "Like Abraham," as he crumpled to the floor.

The women just stared at him.

"Help me drag him into the cooler." Sheila gripped one of the man's skinny ankles.

Darlene stared and tried to wipe the grue from her bosom with napkins.

"Move it!" Sheila barked and Darlene snapped to attention, leaning down and worming her long fingers into the man's hip pocket. Sheila withdrew a key ring, and then grabbed the man's other foot and the two of them dragged him back the aisle to the cooler door.

"What are we gonna do?" Darlene sputtered. "Whose teeth?"

Sheila pushed the dead man into the area

behind the ice machine in the far corner of the cooler. She turned to her friend, put an arm around her shoulder, and leaned close. "We'll sort it out. Go get the mop and bucket and meet me back out front."

Darlene stood and looked at the dead guy who was, up until a few minutes ago, her boss. A man who had a bucket of teeth in his truck. She muttered, "you think you know someone."

Sheila came barreling in. "There's fucking hands in this thing too!" She walked over and kicked the dead man square in the face. His left eye popped from the impact of her toe. "Get the mop and we can clean this shit up.

CHAPTER EIGHT

Sheila walked behind the counter and flipped the switches off for the outside lights by the gas pumps, and then cut half the switches for the overheads in the store.

Darlene gave a soft laugh. "Thank God, we live in a dried up skidmark of a town where no one does nothin'."

"Lock the front, Darlene. Need some time to think."

Sheila's voice had dropped in strength, like a breaking fever. It still had an edge to it, so Darlene did as she was asked, turning the lock on the front door and looking both directions down the empty street. She heard the door to Blevins's office creak open and turned to watch Sheila walk inside.

Mr. Tan stared at the drop ceiling tile with his one remaining eye. Darlene knelt down beside him, careful to avoid the puddle of bloody mess around him, and felt his pockets. A cheap flip-phone, some loose change and his keys. A crumpled pack of Marlboros and a weathered Barlow pocketknife. She tilted the corpse on its side, moved to his rear jeans pocket and pinched what felt like a wallet, before trying to wriggle it loose. With her free hand, Darlene pushed on the man's ribs and leaned him forward slightly. She jerked the wallet free and fell back on her ass as the leather bi-fold fell open against the tiled floor.

Darlene swallowed hard and stared.

CHAPTER NINE

Toby didn't understand the pile of shit he had stepped into. The chilled air of the cooler was getting to him and he knew if it was cold enough in here to keep the beer chilled, it was damned sure cold enough to stiffen his ass up for good.

He rubbed his hands over his arms through his sweatshirt as he stood in the darkness and thought. Blevins, deader than dogshit, wasn't any help.

A bucket of teeth and what in the fuck was a pair of hands doing along with it? What the fuck was going on?

Christ on a crutch, they're kids hands, little fuckin' kids' hands! I've got to figure a way out of here because those two split-bottom bitches out front sure as hell ain't gonna let me out.

He shivered in the blackness. *Fuck.*

Blevins.

Toby turned in the darkness toward where his corpse lay. *Owns the place. Which means he has...*

He pulled his lighter from his pocket and flicked it, spilling piss-yellow light around him. He knelt beside Blevins and patted the pockets of the dead man's khakis. The left side gave a metallic jingle and Toby reached inside to withdraw a half dozen quarters and a token from the VFW along with a key ring. It was a small wire ring with two keys on it. Padlock keys. *Dammit!* The boy pocketed the keys anyway. He looked over to the stack of beer along the side. Toby nodded to himself and turned to the right wall of the cooler. A wall made of tight shelving, holding hundreds of cans and bottles, and behind those, glass doors. Toby smiled.

Chapter Ten

Sheila slid the key into the lock on the lip of the drawer, turned, and then slid open the top-side of Blevins' desk. Two full mini-bottles of Jack Daniels and an all-but empty third lay on top. She smiled and snatched them up, before sliding the drawer closed. She yanked open the deeper drawer beneath it. An issue of *Barely Legal* magazine looked very well read. She pushed it aside and saw a small catalog for girl's clothing—*little* girls.

"Fuckin' sicko." Using a pen, she moved it aside and saw an envelope beneath the magazine. She pulled it free and opened the flap, noticing right away it held a thin stack of bills. "Jackpot, motherfucker." She shook the mailer to make sure she got all the money and pictures fell onto the desk blotter.

Four Polaroids of small children in varying states of undress. All with bright pink cheeks and reddened eyes. A sticky note obscured the bottom half of one of the pictures and scrawled on it were the words *first knucklers*. Sheila glanced up at Darlene, who stood in front of the counter by the dead construction worker. Watching her for a moment, Sheila stuffed the money into the right cup of her bra.

The front drawer on the other side of the desk came next and Sheila slid it open and flinched at the sight. She held her breath as she picked up the plastic-wrapped object from where it rested. She saw the entire bottom of the drawer was filled with tubes of Chapstick. All bright colors and flavors, emblazoned with cartoon smiles and little kid fonts. She smelled grape and watermelon scents but skulking underneath was another smell. Sourly organic. She looked at the thing in her hand and dropped it on the desk. She pulled a letter opener from where it lay and started to unwrap it slowly. The smell was stronger. Pungent and tangy. She felt a grimace devour the lower half of her face just as she folded back the final layer of plastic.

It was a Barbie doll.

It had been wrapped tightly with what looked like clear parcel tape. Beneath, all you could make out was the fake flesh tone plastic of the body. Her hair was matted and gross and the pits of her eyes were caked with dark grime and purple waxy residue. Sheila looked at the plastic wrapping and noted the film coating it. The smell suddenly registered with her, and she realized *exactly* where poor Barbie had been. Sheila gagged and pushed the plastic back over the despicable dildo. Pushing the drawer closed, Sheila set her sights on the last drawer handle at the bottom, and cautiously pulled it open. Her breath caught in her throat for a moment, but she used both hands to lift the loop of string in the drawer and hold it in front of her.

On the length of tan baling twine, strung up like a silver dollar necklace from a beach souvenir shop, were six smallish human ears. Each pair of ears was pierced with matching earrings. The center pair held silver spheres. The second had gold unicorn heads, and the third was accented with small silver lightning bolts. The two ears in the center were gray in color and the pairs warmed to pinker tones as they extended out from there.

Fresher? Oh, my fucking god, it's because they're fresher!

"Darl—" Sheila coughed and swallowed. She gingerly set the necklace down on the top of Blevins's desk like a vomit bag she didn't want to spill. "Darlene, you need to get the fuck in—"

"Sheila! You better come out—"

She glanced back at Darlene and saw the girl sitting on her ass by the dead guy, holding something in one of her hands. Even in the dim light of the store, the girl looked pasty.

"Whatever it is… you… get in here, Darlene."

"Sheila, no, you don't under—"

"Get the fuck in here!" Sheila's scream jolted the young girl and Sheila watched her stand and tiptoe over the body and walk her way.

"What do you think is so goddamn—" Darlene's face was angry but she cut her own words short as she stopped in front of the desk and saw the necklace. She blinked several times.

Sheila wondered if the girl was blowing a fuse in front of her.

"Are those…?" Darlene brought her hand up to her mouth. Her lower lip trembled.

"Yeah." Sheila nodded at the girl. "Whatever you found ain't so fuckin' important now, is it?"

"You tell me, *asshole*." Darlene's eyes became glassy as she shifted her gaze away from the human ears. She tossed the wallet onto Blevins's desk where it flopped open, allowing the light to glint off the badge. "You killed a Fed."

CHAPTER ELEVEN

"What're we gonna do?" Darlene whimpered for the thousandth time in the last five minutes. Sheila shot her a look that was brick heavy and made Darlene wince. "I mean it, What're we..."

The smack across her face was hard enough to make Darlene topple over sideways. She stopped herself from hitting the floor by grabbing the nearest shelf and knocking over some Pringle cans in the process. Sheila stood and leaned into the shorter girl's face.

"Shut your suck hole for *five fucking minutes.* I'm thinking."

Sheila strode towards the register and the large bay window that gave view to the lot out front. It was darker than Satan's ass out there. She looked down at the wallet in her hand. At the badge fastened to the inside of it. At the *not-smiling-but-not-gunshot* face of Mr. Tan whose real name was Agent William Strand.

Sheila thumbed through the wallet, finding a twenty, ten and two ones. Pulling those out, she tucked the money into her bra along with Blevins's cash. The flipside of the badge held his driver's license, and a MasterCard. Behind those, she pulled loose two receipts for Lombardo's Pizzeria and something else fluttered out to the counter top. A photo of a dark-haired girl—ten or eleven, maybe. Pretty little thing with big Bambi eyes and a cute smile with dimples. Had her hair pulled back in a ponytail to show off her earrings.

Small, silver, unicorn head earrings.

Sheila leaned forward enough that her forehead rested against the cool glass.

"Oh, for fuck's sake." She hissed, and let her head to slide down the glass to rest on the counter, leaving a streak on the window from her oily skin. Sheila was on the verge of nodding off from shock and stress, when a loud crash from behind jolted her to attention. She turned quickly and pointed the gun to where Darlene stood staring at the coolers. The fourth door was a large mouth—jagged splinters of glass jutting like teeth. The case of beer that had been thrown through it from inside had busted open on the floor, several cans hissing and foaming.

"Darlene!" Sheila screamed as she watched a leg wearing dirty jeans stretch from the hole in the busted cooler door. Darlene ran from Blevins's office and they watched the boy duck down to fit through the opening and step into the room.

"Fuck you think you're doin', Houdini?" Sheila stepped forward, the pistol pointed at him.

Toby held his hands up. "I… I thought you two had left. I was gonna freeze to—"

"Well we ain't fuckin' gone, now are we, asshole?" Sheila waved the pistol at him. "Sit down! Sit right the fuck down in that corner! Crisscross, applesauce, like a good motherfucker!"

"Okay! All right!" Toby backed up toward the wall and eased himself down to the floor.

Sheila kept the gun trained on him and lowered her voice. "Darlene, c'mere. I need you to do somethin' for me." She waited until Darlene was close and leaned in as if telling her a secret. "I need you to go outside and take a look around in your crush's truck."

"For what?"

Sheila gritted her teeth. "Just fuckin' do it. Look through *everything*. Under the seats, in the glove box. If there's a toolbox in the bed of the pickup, search it like you're lookin' for a winning lotto ticket. I can't tell you what you're lookin' for, but you'll know it when you see it."

Darlene glanced at the boy in the corner. "You'll be okay with him?"

"Who, asshole over there?" Sheila sneered and raised her voice. "Unless he wants to end up like Blevins, he'll be a good boy."

Toby glanced up from rubbing warmth back into his arms, nodded at Sheila's threat, and then stared at the floor again.

Darlene grabbed the Fed's keys from the counter. The cowbell on the front door clanged after she unlocked it and stepped out into the shadows. Sheila smiled and walked to where Toby was sitting. She hunkered down and looked the pale boy in his beady eyes. "How you doin', Cupcake?" She smiled wide and feral.

CHAPTER TWELVE

The punch came faster and harder than Toby intended. He had the keyring in his fist, tiny metal nubs of the padlock keys jutting out from between his fingers when he struck out. The soft flesh of the girl's cheek gave way as the brass punctured her skin. His knuckles followed and connected hard against her jaw. She yowled and dropped the gun as she covered her face to prevent any further damage. Toby swept his leg out and around, kicking the gun towards his crotch where he grabbed it with his left hand. By the time Sheila took her hands down and sneered at him, a tiny extra mouth had torn open on the side of her face. Toby had the gun pointed right at her.

"Howdy." He smiled as he kicked her in the crotch and watched her fall to her knees. "How *you* doin', Cupcake?" He looked down into her widening eyes and smiled a big happy church service smile.

The ding of the cowbell when Darlene came back in tore his attention away for a second, but Toby went back to staring at the prone bleeding girl in front of him when Darlene hollered.

"Sheila, you're not going to *believe* this shit. Not in a million..."

Toby watched Darlene turned the corner and look down at her friend on the floor with a bleeding hole in her face. Darlene's gaze switched to the gun in his hands and then to a manila envelope she held with shaking hands. She shook her head slightly and looked back to him. "Now what?"

Toby took a step away from Sheila and swung the pistol toward Darlene. "Whatcha got there?"

Darlene's gaze flicked to Sheila and back. "Nothin' really. I mean, I don't—"

"Bring it here. Toss it to the floor."

Darlene stepped closer and gave it an underhand toss toward his feet. Toby didn't take his eyes off of her as he knelt down and picked it up. He pulled the contents free of the envelope and only then did he steal a glance away from the two of them. His expression dropped and then hardened before looking back to Darlene. "Fuck's this? Where'd you get this?"

"From the..." She pointed to the dead man on the floor. "From *his* truck. They was shoved in the toolbox behind the seat."

Toby looked back to the sheets of papers, shuffling through until he stopped. His nostrils flared and his eyes reddened. He let the papers fall to the floor and pointed the pistol back out at Darlene and then to Sheila. "Fuck is THIS? What's going on?"

"Toby?" Darlene raised her hands out in front of her. "I don't... *we* don't know what's going on here either, but... it's bad." She kept her hands held up as she walked to the counter, picked up the Fed's wallet where Sheila had left it, and brought it and the photograph toward Toby. She tossed them at his feet.

"Whatever's in those papers are from the dead guy. He's a Fed." Sheila's words sounded slurred with her ruined cheek and she grimaced as she spoke. Tiny red bubbles showed themselves with every drawn-out word.

Toby's eyes drifted down to the badge and the photo of the little girl on the dirty linoleum. His tears stopped and what washed over his face wasn't pain or rage. It was a strange mixture of relief and calm. He swallowed hard. "That... that's my little sister." His voice lowered to a whisper. "She's been missing for the last two months."

"From Steelwater?" Darlene's voice was soft.

Toby nodded. "Just like the girl six months ago and the two girls a year before that." He glared at them. "If you two trailer park whores watched the news once in a while, you'd have heard about it."

CHAPTER THIRTEEN

They all sat in a story-time circle like old friends. Circumstances have a not-too-kind way of leveling the field sometimes. Darlene held an almost-empty roll of paper towels against the ruins of Sheila's cheek, the blood soaking through the cardboard tube in the center. Next to Darlene, Toby knelt and looked at the pictures they had spread out before them. There were over a dozen of them. In every one was a little girl, sometimes dressed, other times not. The only constants in the series were the scuzzy green linoleum, and the fear painted on their cherubic faces.

No one said a word, they just stared at the pictures.

The front door jostled and the cowbell dinged to life, Sheila jumped as did Toby, and Darlene gasped loudly. Sheila held up a finger and whispered. "They'll go away. I made a sign that said we was havin' a power issue and the store was closed. Sorry for the incontinence."

Toby shook his head and felt ashamed of the smile that bloomed. "You meant *inconvenience*. Incontinence is when you can't help but piss or shit yourself."

Darlene giggled. Sheila smiled herself, although it was a ghoulish thing with her torn cheek. "Fuck you, they'll get the idea."

They sat quietly and listened to the door shake as the obviously illiterate bastard outside kept at it. They waited for the silence to return and Toby began moving the pictures into rows resembling a game of Solitaire. "These are girls from Steelwater." He dragged the last one to the third row and laid it under the other two in the column.

"The second row is girls we don't know. This third... These look older than the others. Not the girls, but the pictures." They stared at the pictures some more and after a moment, Darlene pointed to one. A skinny little brown eyed girl lying on the green floor. She had on pink shorts and no shirt. Her little ribs clearly visible. She was all of seven years old. Darlene cleared her throat. "This one."

"What about it? It's just the same as the others, poor little girl half naked on that fuckin' green floor."

"Not quite..." Darlene tapped the corner of the picture with one of her painted claws. "Here. What's that look like to you?"

Toby grabbed the picture and tilted it into the light of the overhead fluorescent. "Oh, my fuckin' God." He whispered the words. "Is that the bottom of a holster, like hanging on a kitchen chair?"

"It might be but I was meaning this right here..." Darlene tapped again, right below the perceived holster. In the bottom right corner there was a small bit of white with a bright blue swoosh. A sneaker. It had a dark spot on the side like paint or something had been spilled on it.

"So, it's a foot. Wearing a fucking Nike. Really narrows it down." Toby snapped.

"Ahem." Sheila nodded towards the dead agent on the floor. They all turned to look and their gaze flowed to his feet. To the white Nike sneakers. To the bright blue swoosh. To the bird shit shaped splotch of grey paint on the side of the left one.

"Fuck me a river." Darlene whispered.

CHAPTER FOURTEEN

They had no idea what shit they'd stepped into but they were all well aware it wasn't coming off their shoes easily. In fact, there was probably a lot more shit on the path ahead.

Toby picked up the pistol, looked at Sheila, and felt a small rush of sympathy for the injury he had dealt her. "I'm sorry again about your face." He shrugged, his eyes averted. "You'll still be pretty as hell even with a little scar."

Sheila shook her head. "Yeah, guess I'll have to drop out of the Miss America pageant this year."

Toby twisted at the waist and removed something from one of the hooks on the pegboard above the lower shelf. He tore the plastic from the backing and let it fall to the floor. "What're you doing?" Darlene asked as he twisted the cap from the miniscule tube in his hand.

Toby smirked and nodded to Sheila. "My history teacher told me this is what they invented this shit for initially. He was obsessed about the war in Vietnam. Said the military invented both super glue and duct tape for med kits in combat. The tape can seal a wound damned near airtight and keep them from bleeding out until they get to a hospital. Then, a while after, they invented the glue. When they saw the way it bonds to skin they decided it was even better than the tape."

The boy scooched closer to Sheila and took the blood-soaked roll of towels away from her cheek. The wound dribbled fresh lines of blood down

Sheila's cheek. Toby knew, as deep as the punctures were, they weren't going to clot any time soon. Sheila looked at him with wide eyes. He held the tube between surprisingly steady fingers.

"Hon, as much as that has hurt you this last hour, this ain't gonna be but a flea bite. Hold her hands, Darlene. And Sheila? Don't move a muscle in that pretty face of yours. I'm just gonna sploot some of this over the cut and gently smear it to coat the whole thing. It dries in an instant. It will sting, well, maybe closer to burn." He nodded to the younger girl.

Darlene gripped the other girl's hands in hers and squeezed them tight. Sheila's eyes watered as the glue touched raw meat and flayed skin but she did not cry out. After squeezing a liberal dollop on the wound, Toby used the end of the tube like a putty knife to smooth the glue over the jagged holes and blew air on it to dry.

He dropped the tube and the towels to the floor and sat back. "All done." He smiled and turned to the other side of the aisle and jammed a fist into one of the colorful boxes there. He pulled back with a lollipop jutting from his fist. "A good girl gets a treat." Sheila smacked it from his hand and rolled her eyes at him.

Toby lifted the gun in his hand. "We got any more ammo for this thing?"

CHAPTER FIFTEEN

"You didn't really come in here to rob the place tonight, did you?" Darlene had her arms crossed in front of her as she stared at Toby. Something didn't quite fit right about it all. He wasn't a tweaker—looked poor, but not desperate enough to turn to robbing. Aside from the too baggy clothes and slightly crazy eyes, he looked like any other kid about to graduate high school.

Toby was studying the photographs laid out on the floor and shook his head. "That wasn't the plan, no. I saw Blevins's truck here and it's why I came in, to go after him, but I got inside and you two were here and Mister…" He motioned with the pistol toward the dead agent. "Asshole over there, and I panicked because I didn't see Blevins. Didn't know he was already…" He put the pistol down to his side and looked from Darlene to Sheila and back again. "Why in the fuck is Blevins dead anyway?"

Sheila let her gaze drift to the floor and shrugged. "Shit happens."

"Shit…" He gave a bitter laugh. "Shit happens? That's all you got?"

Darlene shifted in place. "Why were you coming after Blevins?"

"You've heard the rumors. I know damned well you have. Can't work at this store without hearin' them. Blevins likes 'em young." Toby tucked the pistol into the waistband of his jeans.

"I mean… yeah, we've both heard it, but never seen him do nothin' out of line." Darlene shook her head.

"Since my sister went missing, I started asking around town. People talk in Steelwater, you know how it is. Everybody knows everybody. The more I asked, the more people whispered. Led me here."

"Wouldn't put it past that pencil-dick motherfucker, though." Sheila worked her jaw and winced. "Not like he stood a chance with a grown woman."

Toby stood up, walked toward the corpse, and stood over him. "And what exactly were *you* doing in the goddamn photograph?" He turned toward Darlene. "You got Blevins's keys?"

"Truck is unlocked and I already looked in it." Sheila spoke up. "That's where I found the bucket of... the bucket."

"Any other keys to anything on it? His house? Closet in his office? Anything?"

Sheila pulled the keyring from her pocket and held it up in front of her. "This is the shop keys. Nothing on it but the keys to the front, his office door, and the rear wells. His desk..."

"I'm guessin' you two Dollar Tree Detectives already checked that shit out?"

Darlene winced and Sheila's face went a lighter shade of green. She jacked a thumb to the back room. "I didn't lock it back up, so go git a look for yourself."

The young man walked to the rear area of the store, and Darlene saw the light flicker on. The clunking noise of the desk drawers being opened. Papers being flung about.

"Jesus fuck! Did he lube this thing with kiddie Chapstick?"

Darlene turned to Sheila, who shook her head and waved a hand at her questioning expression.

Toby's exclamation was followed by a sound so loud it could be nothing short of Toby tipping the desk over.

Darlene hadn't even seen him return to the aisle they were in until his voice ruptured the silent web cocooning them.

"What rear wells?" Toby took a step closer.

"The old fuel tanks behind the building, but they ain't been used in... hell, since before I started workin' here four years ago. Maybe even longer." Sheila tossed the keys to Toby and then reached out to the shelf in front of her. She grabbed a bag of barbecue chips and pulled the top apart in a practiced move.

Toby watched her as she popped a few into her mouth and crunched. "You're gonna regret that as soon as the salt hits your—"

Sheila yowled like an alley cat and brought her hand up to the opaque scab of pink glue marring her cheek.

Toby shook his head and turned back to Darlene. "Not used in over four years, huh?"

Darlene shook her head. "Not that I know of. State made him put in them new environmental tanks back then and he was to have the old filled with sand or somethin'. But I've seen Blevins messing around with them sometimes at night when I'm out... you know... messing around and stuff."

"Tell me something, girls." Toby held the keys out in front of him. "If the tanks haven't been used in so long... why in the hell would Blevins still keep the keys up close and personal on him?"

Darlene's focus turned to the keys swinging like a pendulum from Toby's hand.

He peered at her from the dangling brass. "Up for a little field trip, ladies?"

Chapter Sixteen

There were four lids in the far back lot. The area had been virtually ignored except as a salvage yard/dumping ground for Blevins and his *Sanford and Son* pals for the last half decade. Toby pulled away a sun-faded kiddie pool, the once bright-blue sides now bleached a dull bone color. Underneath it was a manhole cover, much larger than a normal street version, with a number 1 spray painted on the dirty cement around the edge.

Toby looked along the weeds at the back wall of the store and pulled a length of rusted rebar from a pile of warped plywood. He leaned down at the manhole, worked the rebar into a slotted hole along the edge, and leveraged his weight until the lid shifted up from the opening. Toby slid it aside and they all leaned forward to peer down as Darlene flicked on the flashlight she had grabbed from the store.

Sand. The tunnel went down about three feet before it became nothing but sand. Toby sighed and dragged the lid back in place, stood, and dragged the pool back in place.

Sheila pointed toward the next lid and they walked a few paces to a stack of wooden pallets. Darlene and Toby set about pulling them away, sending a group of black crickets in search of fresh cover. Toby crouched and pried the lid off as he had before.

Sheila took the light this time and shined it down the mouth of the tunnel. "Well, fuck me."

The ladder went down farther than it did in the other. From the angle, they could see nothing but stuffed animals and dolls below. Dirty pink toy bunnies and faded orange duckies. Floppy ears and glass eyes. Little plastic arms and legs jutting from spaces between. The trio stood there staring into the maw, the moon shining down like a spotlight on a prison yard.

"You said there was another one?" Toby dragged the cover back in place, once again bringing darkness to the tomb of toys.

"Over there behind that old soda machine. Under them crates." Sheila motioned in the direction with her flash light and the trio moved as one across the patch of cracked asphalt and weeds. The night was still and every sound seemed amplified. Toby moved the stack of wooden crates, letting them fall on their sides. He kicked away the damp cardboard covering the lid. Under the weak light, the fleeing insects shimmered like tiny eyes. He edged the pry bar under the lid and lifted. A thick acrid stink smacked them hard as they leaned forward. Urine mixed with something else—something familiar but unpleasant.

CHAPTER SEVENTEEN

Toby put his hands against the asphalt and started climbing down the ladder. He reached the bottom and aimed the flashlight upward for Darlene and Sheila to follow. When they reached bottom, he turned the beam of light on the enclosure. It was bigger than he expected—roughly eighteen by eighteen feet—and he had a feeling this well had never seen a drop of fuel since it had been built.

One cement wall had a backdrop duct taped to it, a canvas of mottled gray like the ones used in yearbook photos. A tripod and video camera rested several feet away on the filthy green linoleum floor. The corners of the vinyl were curling and cracked where it fell short of covering the entire floor. Old clothing was clotted in piles there, mixed among it were old soup cans, bottles and more filthy toys. A wash of the light showed sparkly designs and lots of pink. Some mottled with mold. The far corner, nearest the camera, was littered with fast food wrappers and pizza boxes and small sneakers. An old kitchenette set sat off to the other side of the room. Red Formica top with three chairs sporting sparkly red cushions and backs.

"That's the chair from the photograph the Fed is in." Darlene's expression was beyond disgusted.

The place smelled wild. Stagnant. Funky with rot and damp and the smell of—

"What the hell is this place?" Darlene had her arms crossed over her chest. She looked like she was trying to shield herself from getting contaminated.

"You know exactly what it is." Toby stepped toward the small table and chairs. An overflowing ashtray rested on its top. Stubs of cigarettes, cigars and a few burnt roaches filled the plastic tray. A box of wooden matches guarded it. A torn issue of *Hustler* magazine and a *My Little Pony* coloring book with a handful of broken Crayons. A ratty teddy bear and two bottles of pink nail polish.

Sheila kicked at something on the floor, flinched, and gagged. A pair of purple jeans—small, damp and smelling of piss. Her chest began to tighten and she grabbed Darlene's hand and squeezed. Darlene looked at her and swallowed hard, nodding.

Toby swung the light to see an old green couch with torn cushions. A bottle of Banker's Club vodka and a can of Hawaiian punch were on the floor in front of it. There was a *Dora The Explorer* cup tipped over near a coagulated puddle of bright red.

Darlene's footsteps shuffled in the mess and there was a crackling sound as an overhead fluorescent light snapped on. It shed a cold light across the room, somehow making it worse than the yellow glow of Toby's flashlight, but he clicked it off anyway. Small black dots with tiny legs scattered like buckshot in the new illumination.

A low wooden cabinet sat in the corner closest to the ladder and Toby stepped toward it. A short stack of manila folders sat on top and he flipped the top folder open. Photos of a young girl were on top of other papers that looked like a model's résumé. *Body measurements. Hair color. Eye color.* Toby's stomach rolled and he flipped the folder shut. It was dusty, and most of the paperwork looked as though it had been there a while—peppered with mildew and roach shit and wavy from dampness.

"These fuckers. These… fucking… motherfuckers!" His grip tightened on the pistol and he wanted to fire it badly, wanted to shoot the place up full of holes, but he knew it wouldn't do anything at all except make the three of them deaf for an hour.

A shifting noise came from the far side of the room and the three of them spun toward the sound. Two hands reached over the rear cushion of the green sofa.

Small hands.

A *child's* hands.

Nails painted bright blue and glittery.

"Oh my God!" Darlene gasped and let go of Sheila as both girls started toward the sofa. Toby cocked a head and squinted his eyes a little. "Ladies, I think we need to be a little more…"

The lights went out.

Sheila screamed—a rough, gravelly sound tearing from her throat.

Toby frantically flicked the switch on the flashlight to no avail. "Darlene stay still! Sheila?" His voice was unsteady. He took a few steps in the direction of the couch. He heard the whisper of feet through garbage followed by another sound, like a child's laughter. He held the flashlight up and tried the switch once more.

When the light came on, it was Toby's turn to scream.

CHAPTER EIGHTEEN

The man standing in front of him was inches from Toby's face. The stranger's face bristled with a coat of whiskers and he wore a grease-spotted John Deere hat. His eyes were wide and bloodshot as he stared at Toby with a finger held up across his lips. His eyes darted like nervous vermin. *"Shhhhhhhhhh."*

Toby took a step backward, and he brought the pistol up in front of him. "Who the fuck're you?"

The man shook his head slightly, and repeated the hushing noise. *"Shhhhh."* He nodded in the direction of the couch and mouthed the words *be quiet*.

"I'm the one with the *fuckin' gun* so I wouldn't be telling me to quiet down, you sick fuck." Toby's stomach shook inside, adrenaline flushed through his bloodstream. He felt dangerously close to muddying his britches.

Darlene was frozen in place, her arms tight around her body. Sheila shifted in place and Toby watched her take a step toward the tripod, likely to use it as a weapon.

"You don't wanna do that." The man whispered softly and calmly, a whispered monotone as he held his arms out slightly to his sides, a six-pack of Budweiser in his right hand and a crumpled bag from McDonald's in the other. "I'm not a threat." He nodded toward the rear of the room. "She is."

The soft giggling of the child had stopped and the sound coming from behind the filthy sofa had grown deeper, thickening to a low rumbling growl, like a cat purring over a loudspeaker.

"*Shhhh. Shhhhhhhh.* Abby, it's okay. Easy now." The man slowly put the six-pack on the table and straightened again. Toby noticed then the deep grooves scratched into the Formica top of the table. The stranger patted the air and spoke. "Settle down, now. It's okay, Hun."

Toby took another step away, turning so he could keep his pistol trained on the man and safely glance at the sofa.

From the right edge of the sofa, a small hand curled around the cushion. It was followed by a sliver's view of a face, and an eye peering around the green cushions.

Toby felt his muscles turn to water and he lowered the pistol to his side.

The child moved—*no, she scampered*—from the sofa, and ran toward the man, curling around his legs like a scared animal. The whole distance of maybe seven feet eaten in a blur.

She was clothed in a yellow sleeveless blouse with a flower pattern. Torn jeans covered her bottom half and the entire outfit was stained with splotches of varying colors. One thin wrist had a bracelet on it made of large colorful beads shaped like hearts.

But what held Toby's attention was her face and head. There was no doubt it was a girl child, with the soft angles and full lips. Her hair was pure white, fading to disgust and tangled filth as it reached the ends of the oily strands.

She grunted and moved around to the other side of the man and he reached down and ran a hand over the top of her head. She rubbed against him as a cat would, relishing the affection, until he pulled away again. "Be still, Abby." He nodded toward the new arrivals. "We got company."

That was when she stared at Toby, her eyes full and wide and predatory. Eyes, from edge to edge, as black as the bottom of a coalmine, save for the pinpricks of blood red pupils.

CHAPTER NINETEEN

The man in the greasy cap pointed to the dilapidated couch and made a *snicking* noise with his teeth. The girl-thing tilted her angular face up to his and moved rapidly as he snapped his fingers and kept pointing. She lunged across the floor in two large leaps, up and over the sofa, disappearing into the pocket of shadow behind the furniture.

The man looked at Toby and the girls and spoke softly but plainly. "I'm going to feed her, and when I say *Now*, you kids git up that ladder quickly and quietly. I'll be right behind you." He scratched at a scab just below his left eye. "I'm sort of glad to see ya."

He took a few steps toward the couch, tore the side of the brown bag open, and holding the bag over the back of the sofa, shook free of the carton French fries and three burgers wrapped in yellow paper. He crumbled the bag with practiced precision and lobbed it into the corner with the other garbage. He stood still and the only sounds were of ripping paper and moist chewing. The man leveled his gaze at Toby and whispered. "Now."

CHAPTER TWENTY

In all the horror movies Darlene had ever seen, this would have been the part where they clamber up the rusty ladder rungs, a beast hot on their heels, snapping and snarling as they barely made it to safety. The reality was that didn't happen. The three of them made it up and out into the back lot of the store with ease. They stood and stared down the chute like it was a gullet about to vomit up some nasty bit of gristle.

The darkness was breached by a patch of green as the man with the dirty hat rose from the opening. He leaned and dragged the heavy steel lid back in place and began replacing the cardboard.

Darlene watched him freeze in place when the click of a gun being cocked broke the silence. He slowly straightened, turned to face the trio, and sighed.

"It ain't what you think."

Toby sneered and raised the gun a little higher. "You mean you weren't in cahoots with the fuck that owns this dump and who knows who the hell else, makin' kiddie porn and diddling little girls?"

The man removed his rancid hat and wiped an arm across his forehead. His eyes looked wet and he cleared his throat. "Ok. Then... it ain't *exactly* what you think." He sniffled and spat something on the ground that glistened like a precious stone.

Darlene's stomach turned.

He put his hat back on and looked at the boy with the gun. "Can we get inside and I'll tell you a story?"

Toby glanced at the girls and Sheila nodded, though she looked like she had been making out with a hive full of hornets—wound sealed shut or not, the right side of her face was a swollen mess. "You in front. Walk to the door." The man took the lead and Toby tapped his lower back with the nose of the gun. "No fuckin' around, pal. We got a body count we ain't afraid to add to."

Darlene stood rooted in the lot, stared at the manhole cover and wondered about the thing in the hole devouring its snack.

CHAPTER TWENTY-ONE

"Ok, Mister. Shoot." Toby glanced at the gun in his hand and smiled at his own terrible pun.

"CJ is what they call me... short for Cracker Joe. That's what they call me. You can go with that."

Toby sucked air through his teeth. "I don't give a dead dog's dick *what* they call you. You said you was gonna spill the story, now do it. We got fifteen shades of mess here to contend with and you and your goddamn Morlock or whatever she is down there is adding to it."

"What the fuck is a Morlock?" Darlene piped up from where she stood near the door.

"It's them swampy places in England." Sheila retorted with swarthy confidence.

Toby sighed and shook his head slowly. "That's the moors." Toby sneered at Darlene. "The Morlocks were these monsters that lived underground in *The Time Machine*. They ate people."

"I don't like books." Darlene made a face like she smelled a fart.

"They made movies of it. The Rex Harrison one is the best." CJ leaned forward as he spoke up, almost childlike in his excitement at the topic.

"You can shut the hell up about the movies. And you two keep it zipped." Toby whirled around on CJ once more. "Now, tell us what in the furry fuck is going on here."

CJ leaned back against the counter and crossed his arms. He glanced at the corpse on the floor and winced. Toby caught his reaction.

"You know the Fed?"

"Fed?" CJ released a harsh laugh and shook his head. "He's no Federal Agent. That badge is faker than Pam Anderson's tits. He just used it to get laid. He was... he was part of everything."

Toby ran through it in his mind, the papers, the photos, the files the man had in his truck. He gritted his teeth and looked at the dead man in disgust.

"Well then..." Darlene put her hands on the counter. Her expression showed nothing but outright disgust. "Nobody innocent has been killed yet." She grabbed a pack of Marlboro Lights from the rack, packed it against her palm, opened it, and then shook one free. *"Yet."* She pulled a lighter from the almost empty rack and lit the cigarette.

"Darlin,' I ain't seen innocent in a month of Sundays." CJ's gaze flickered to Toby before he focused on the floor. "Maybe it's been dog years. What is it, seven for every one?" He stuck the tip of his tongue out and touched it to his thumb, wiped the tiny dab of snuff on his shirt. "Guess he got what was comin' to him. Guess I prolly will, too." He let out a long exhale and tainted the air around him sour wintergreen.

"Started, I guess... 'bout a half-dozen years ago or so. Blevins called me up one afternoon. Supposed to be a poker night. He and I and a few other fellas would get together once every few weeks or so and play cards, drink a little, sometimes smoke a little of this and that." He cleared his throat. "Anyway, Blevins called me and said he was gonna cancel poker night but I should come over to the store about nine o'clock as he was closing early. Wouldn't tell me why, but he seemed... *excited* about something. I thought *great*, he's gonna wanna watch skin flicks. Last thing I wanna see is that dickweed punching his dummy again. Thing looks like a shaved hamster someone stretched too thin..." CJ chuckled and then went serious.

"See, I knew Blevins from way back, high school even. Always was a bit odd and kept to himself, but hell, so did I. Wasn't like back then, he was—"

Toby shifted in place and crossed his arms, the pistol still tightly in his grip. "Let's skip the glory days and get to the goddamn point, yeah?"

CJ nodded without looking up.

Sheila opened a fresh bag of potato chips, the cellophane loud in the silence. She shrugged as they watched her stuff a chip into the undamaged side of her mouth.

"I got to the store here just before nine o'clock, in time to see the pump lights go dark and Blevins come walking outside. He had this strange smile on his face, like he was a kid on Christmas Eve. I followed him out back o' the store and he used a crowbar to pop off the top of the well."

"I thought them wells was still holdin' gas back then?" Toby spoke.

"All but the far one, one we was just in. That'n was always empty from the get go."

CJ slid his finger between his bottom lip and teeth and flung the wad of wet snuff onto the linoleum. Darlene grimaced as CJ eased a hand into his front shirt pocket, withdrawing a can of Kodiak. He popped the lid and pinched some in his fingers, and then packed it behind his bottom lip. "He had a girl in there, the daughter of that attorney from East End, one that was caught takin' money from the contractors for pushing approvals through the township."

"Abigail Wilson." Toby remembered the girl's name from asking people around town. She had been the first girl in the area to go missing, barely six years old at the time.

"Bingo." CJ nodded and pointed a finger at Toby.

End him. End this motherfucker right now. Put a bullet in his forehead and leave him to rot where he falls.

Toby's grip tightened on the pistol.

Oh, God, it would feel so good to stop a piece of shit like this from even breathing the same air as me.

Toby swallowed hard and forced his hand to relax. He had to know the rest. "And then? What happened then, you son of a bitch?"

CHAPTER TWENTY-TWO

"We went down the hole, and he already had it set up like a little apartment or something. I knew as soon as he turned on the lights it was fucked up. I mean, it was thought out and shit. The little girl was sitting at the table, eating a bowl of macaroni and cheese, the bright yellow shit you make from a box. Hell, that ain't no mac and chee—"

"Fucking focus!" Toby snarled and stomped a foot. It seemed a silly gesture but Toby needed the man to get back on track. He needed answers.

CJ coughed and nodded.

"I asked him what was up. Blevins smiled and said he was gonna teach that 'ttorney a hard lesson. And while he had her, maybe that weren't all the hard lessons that could be had. He smiled and it made my stomach drop. I ain't never had an attraction to kids. I had heard about Blevins but never saw nothin' to prove it as fact. Not until that night. I told him I was leaving. I didn't want no part of whatever he was cooking up. When I turned to go back up I heard him pump the shotgun. He said I was with him whether I wanted to be or not. I stood there and listened to his plan. And my God, what a vile thing it was..." CJ stopped and nodded to the cooler nearest him. "Can I nick a drink?"

"Go on." Toby glanced at Sheila and gave her a nod before looking back to CJ. Sheila walked to the cooler and withdrew a sweet tea, stepping over and handing it over.

The filthy man uncapped it and guzzled half

the bottle, and then brought an air of class to the joint with a rumbling belch. He gave a weak smile and cleared his throat before he resumed speaking.

"Blevins' master plan was simple. He kidnapped the girl and hoped to ransom her in exchange for Daddy's cooperation on a few things." CJ paused and his mouth swerved into a smirk as he stared into the air, peeling away layers of time. "Least it *would have* been simple had her Daddy ever contacted us back. Hell, they never even did an investigation worth a pinch o' shit. I mean, this might be a fuckin' Dogpatch town but even Barney fuckin' Fife could have found the girl. But she went gone--Blevins snatched her from her own front yard in broad ass daylight!? So yeah, she was gone and we sent a note and made the ransom calls and shit and we got almost no response at all. We didn't get it. Not right away, at least."

CJ's eyes glassed over and Toby wasn't sure if it was from guilt or something else entirely. The man's next words were softer, almost as if he didn't want to say them out loud.

"But then… the girl hadn't shown her true self yet."

CHAPTER TWENTY-THREE

A silver sedan pulled into the parking lot, slowed as it went past the gas pumps, and Toby watched as it gunned out of the lot, spinning gravel behind it.

"I think he knew. *Somehow,* he knew what she would become. Shit, maybe what she already was." CJ spit a wad of brown juice to the floor.

Sheila crumpled the now empty bag of chips and let it fall. "And what is that, huh? What exactly *is* she? 'Cause I ain't never seen anythin' with eyes like that."

"You're all from Steelwater, yeah? Raised here?"

They all nodded at CJ. "Growin' up, you had to have heard tale of the ol' lady livin' out in the wetlands, out past the quarry in that old shack."

Toby took a swallow of tea and rested the bottle on a shelf next to boxes of Pop-Tarts. "Oh, come the fuck on. That's bullshit. The ol' *muck witch?*" His own mother had tried to scare him with the tales when he was a kid. He hadn't believed it back then, either.

CJ nodded and smiled. "My momma went to her after I was born. Couldn't stop bleedin' and didn't want to go to the hospital. Ol' woman whispered some words and did some things, made my *momma* do some things... well, they weren't exactly *Christian*, if you know what I mean. Fixed her right up though."

"So?" Sheila put her fingers to her wounded

cheek and winced. The patch of dried glue shimmered in the dull light.

CJ shifted in place. "*So*... I think... hell, I *know* she had something to do with it. Something to do with that lawyer man. With makin' that girl the way she is. Maybe jus' with makin' the girl... period."

"What, like a trade? Sell your soul at the crossroads shit?" Toby shook his head and felt the weight of the pistol in his hands. He could feel his anger start to rise again, listening to this man's bullshit.

"Somethin' like that, yeah. That fat-assed lawyer's a millionaire because of every back alley deal he made in this town. Everything lined up for him. Ducks in a goddamn row. *Every. Goddamn. Thing.* There's luck and there's greased palms and then there's this. And not a goddamn word about his daughter gone missing. No *cops*. No *FBI*. No *nothin'* to search for her at all. Just acceptance, like she was *supposed* to go missin' at some point. Like he *expected* it to happen."

"Or like he managed to get rid of somethin'." Darlene mumbled, and it was ignored by the others.

"I recall seein' on the news about the search for her so that ain't all true." Sheila spoke for the first time in what seemed like hours.

CJ shook his head. "Nah. You saw what *looked* like a search. You saw guys in orange, truckin' through the fields and woods. You saw bouncing flashlight beams... but all you saw was some shit on the TV. Fuck, that little box is the biggest liar of them all. We faked landing on the moon so a fake search for a missing kid is easy as pie."

CJ reached for his iced tea. "Week or so went by and some bullshit story came out about finding the girl dead in a culvert pipe, 'cept Blevins and I knew different."

"The attorney made a cover story about his own daughter?" Darlene stubbed out her cigarette on the counter top and reached for the pack again, lighting another one on the heels of the first.

CJ nodded. "I'm sure the ol' boys club were all in on it. Buried an empty casket up in St. Michael's cemetery. Had a hell of a crowd from what I recall."

Silence hung heavy in the room and then Toby broke it.

"And the others? Or haven't we hit that part of your fuckin' fairytale yet?" Toby gritted his teeth. "What about the other girls that went missing? What about my little sister?"

CJ glanced at him, and then found the floor yet again. "Your sister... I... I didn't... Son, I'm—"

Toby stepped forward and jammed the barrel of the pistol into the side of CJ's face. "Call me *Son* again! Call me *Son* one more fuckin' time!"

CJ put his hands up in surrender. "I'm sorry. I didn't know one of them was your sister..." The man's face scrunched up with emotion. "We *had* to... you don't understand. We *had* to—"

The man's left hand came down like a copperhead strike, right at the same time he jerked his head away from the line of the pistol barrel. One moment, Toby held the heavy weapon in his hand

and the next, it had vanished.

CJ held the pistol in his filthy hand, the business end aimed at Toby's face. His expression had gone serious again, no trace of emotion. "Sit the fuck down... *Son*."

CHAPTER TWENTY-FOUR

"Ok, boy and girls.... it seems we got ourselves a… *situation*." CJ smiled and a trickle of spit ran down a crease in his fat chin. "All of what I told you is true, 'cept the parts that ain't." He smiled again and it was a doorway to bad news.

He pursed his lips and sucked against his front teeth as he turned to Toby. "I didn't know it was your little sister, but truth be told, I wouldn't have cared much, neither. Kiddie split is kiddie split, and while it ain't my cuppa tea, them sickos that's in for that shit pay good *good* money. So, when the girl started changing and we got our *instructions* we figured out a way to make it work for us a little. Blevins realized his kidnapping scenario was shot to shit. He was just about ready to tie her up and take her back to Daddy when the phone rang."

CJ paused again, like a cub scout leader tying his charges up with a ghost story, "And speak of the goddamned devil—it was *Daddy* on the line. When he got done laughin' at us, he told us what we was in for… Abigail wasn't even his daughter. Fuckin' dude *had* no kids. She was the lien against his debt. See, he got everything he wanted if he kept her… *it*…and kept her fed and happy. An' if'n you keep her fed, she's a sweet little thing." He levelled a leer at Sheila and smirked. "Her tongue is sandy an' feels like a kitten's."

Toby's guts churned at the words. He considered leaping at the son of a bitch, but didn't.

"You stop feeding her or try to get rid of her,

an' she's like a bad penny and a case of the clap. You think you're in the clear but that ain't the case." CJ took a gulp of his tea, finishing it, tossed the plastic bottle over his shoulder, and looked at Darlene. "First night after the 'ttorney told us this shit and we realized we weren't gonna get paid, we tied her up and took her out to the quarry. Blevins tied a cinder block to her legs—like that crazy church lady from town done her boy some years back—and threw her in. He watched until the air bubbles stopped breaking water. We got back to the station, an' there she was, a waitin' on us. Standing there, right in front of the register, rope still tied around her leg and had a fucking fish in her hand she'd eaten the head off o'..." He stared off in the distance, lost in the recollection, and then shook it away and came back around. He cleared his throat and spit on the floor again. The sour smell of snuff spit wafted in the small area. "I saw Blevins's truck outside, so where's that sumbitch at anyway?"

Darlene and Sheila looked sheepish, like kids caught stealing penny candy. Toby nodded toward the cooler.

CJ grinned. "The cooler? You got him in there freezin' his balls off?"

"Would be if his blood was still pumpin' through his veins." Toby eyed the pistol in the man's grip. *Dumb. So goddamn dumb to let him grab the pistol.*

CJ grunted. He didn't look sad about the news.

"What about the bucket of teeth? What about the necklace of ears?" Sheila's questions came out in a rush.

"When she eats, she don't leave much. Most of it we'd put in a box or a bag and take around to the parks at night and burn 'em up in the fire pits. But teeth can be identified, so we picked them outta the mess. Saved them until we could figure out what the fuck to do with 'em." He sniffed and spat a blob of snot on the floor.

"Why kids?" Darlene stared at the floor as she asked the question, then her gaze lifted.

CJ snorted. "Why kids? Who the hell wants to tangle with one of these good ol' boy rednecks in town? Bigger meal, sure, but bigger threat on the hunt." He shook his head.

"As for them ears, it was a present Abby made for Blevins. She made it herself with some yarn she had down there, prolly from one of the girl's hair and them ears she must've saved. She even spoke when she gave it to him, called him *Papa*. Cute as hell, it was." He coughed and glanced toward the cooler shelves with the beer.

"I'll get you one." Darlene walked from around the counter, not waiting for a response from him. She pulled two tall-boy Budweiser cans from the rack and popped the top on one before handing a can over to him.

"Well ain't you sweet as peach pie?" CJ took the cold beer from her with a smile, his eyes barely leaving the lines of her cleavage.

Darlene shrugged. "Well, I mean… you've got the gun."

He slurped beer and nodded at her. "*Thass* right. Thass *goddamn* right. I *do* have the gun now, don't I?"

Darlene took the other beer with her and stood behind the counter again.

"So, what now?" Sheila's words sounded slurred and Toby figured glue or no glue, the wound in her cheek was stiffening up.

CJ took another slurp. "What now? I'll tell you what now. I'm gonna enjoy this icy and refreshing King of Beers and then it's going to be feeding time again. Go ahead and try to run if'n you want. Don't matter much to her if'n you're alive or dead. It's all just the same. Ya'll are *meat*."

Toby leaned back against the shelf of candy bars and crossed his arms. He heard a shocked breath come from Darlene, but what broke the silence was the sound of Sheila giggling. Then her giggling got louder.

"Fuck're you laughin' at, you crazy slit?" CJ paused from his beer, watching her.

Sheila shook her head, tears from laughing leaking from the corners of her eyes. "You're just a redneck bitch." Her laughter exploded, her whole body shaking with the action.

"*Fuck* did you call me?" CJ's hand tightened on the pistol as Toby watched.

"I called you..." Sheila wiped at her tears. "*A. Redneck. Bitch.*"

CJ put the beer down on the counter and closed the distance of the room, the pistol rising as he did. "Like I said, dead 'r alive, don't matter much."

"Well, it's true, ain't it? That fat assed lawyer got everything *he* wanted. Big house, lots o' money.

Nice car. Bet he's even got a young bitch on his arm ridin' him every night like a buckin' bronco, and *you*... you dumb redneck, are stuck doing all the dirty work for him. Livin' in a fuckin' shithole slinging Big Macs at a monster." Sheila's laughter faded and she stared the man down.

CJ stopped in front of her, opened his mouth to say something and closed it again.

"Don't seem very right, now does it? Look at you. Wearin' greasy jeans and a Sanyo wristwatch. And that truck o' yours out there was old as fuck when I was still swimmin' in my daddy's ball sack. You're just a shit town redneck, bustin' your ass for other people to make 'em rich." Sheila reached for a new bag of sour cream potato chips, taking her time to rip open the top as she stared at CJ. "And *that*... makes *you*... a *bitch*."

CJ whipped the pistol across the already damaged side of her face and Toby watched the glued seam tear open again like a bloody Ziplock top. Sheila hissed with the pain as her head snapped to the side, but she turned her head slowly back and glared at the man.

Toby stepped forward and CJ spun toward him, the gun barrel leveled at his chest. "You want some too, fucker? Try me, hero."

Toby put his hands up. "Wait... easy." He nodded toward Sheila and lowered his voice, forcing it to be calm and steady. "She's right though. You said the girl was a lien against a debt. Or payment for some... process. Why are *you* taking care of it while he gets off scot-free? Don't you want a life of your own? Or you want to be tied down, takin' care of a... whatever she is? Hell, she ain't even your own."

"Not like she's your blood or nothin'." Darlene's voice was timid from behind the counter.

CJ's eyes flickered and he spit on the floor.

"Way I see it is you've got two choices if it's like you say it is with her bein' a bad penny and all." Toby glanced at Sheila and saw the blood seeping from her cheek. "You can return her to that fat assed attorney. Or return her to the ol' witchy bitch and let her collect what's due all these years."

CJ shook his head. "That one ain't an option. The Muck Witch died a while back. You think Blevins and I is stupid? That was one of the first things we tried after Daddy Lawyer called. We rode out to her shack and there she was, swollen like a balloon with one foot blacker'n Sammy Davis's asshole. Gangrene. She could grapple with the darkest of forces but she couldn't keep her sugar in line. Ain't that a pisser?" CJ shook his head.

Sheila opened and closed her mouth, working the muscles. "There's a third choice you can make."

CJ turned back to her. "And what's that, smart ass?"

Keep. Being. A bitch." Sheila pulled a potato chip from the bag she held and pushed it in her mouth, crunching on the snack despite the blood running down her cheek.

CHAPTER TWENTY-FIVE

CJ lunged at the girl, pistol raised above his head like the jawbone of an ass. He started the downswing as Toby leapt at him and knocked him off balance. CJ fell into the wire rack of beef jerky and pickled sausages. Jars of assorted meats shattered open and littered the aisle. The bigger man grabbed for the gun sliding across the tile, barely missing it. Sheila dove, landing flat against the floor, and the gun stopped against her ample bosom. She grabbed it and jumped up, gun trained on CJ.

"Freeze, dick licker!" The two men ceased their wrestling and Toby mashed the other man's face into the floor as he pushed himself up. He sniffed back the trickle of blood from his own nose and spat on the foul green hat lying at his feet. CJ managed to get himself righted and knelt, swaying a little as his breathing slowed. His left eye was a swollen mess and his nose would never be straight again, but he would live. He looked at the girl with the gun and wheezed a deep wretched breath.

"I'll tell ya, Sugartits... you sure beat all, you know that? I mean, Goddamn, you're ballsy as fuck. And we'll talk about them sweater puppies some other time." CJ winked with his good eye and started to laugh. It devolved into a tittering whimpering sound, until his eyes rolled up into his head and he fainted dead away, thumping against the floor.

Toby looked at the girls and they all looked at the crumpled heap of redneck, surrounded by pickled meats, broken glass, and speckles of blood. The store was silent save for the small sound of breathing and the hum of the ventilation system.

After a long moment, Darlene spoke, dead pan. "Well, that was something."

Toby opened his mouth to speak when the long window behind the counter cracked. A lightning bolt zig-zag halved the surface. The lights went out in the building and Toby pulled the flash light he still had in his back pocket. The beam cut through the darkness and washed over the glass and the night behind it, but only for a second, and then it too went out. They stared at the slab of oily black window and Sheila gasped as a pair of small red dots appeared on the other side of it, seeming to reflect the very shadows of the night to brighten their vermillion hue.

CHAPTER TWENTY-SIX

Toby swallowed hard, his gaze never leaving the small silhouette outside the glass. "Darlene?" He voice was a whisper. "Did anyone lock the front door when we came in?"

In his periphery, Toby saw Darlene's focus was as trained on the shadow as he was.

"I don't know. I don't remember." Darlene's voice trembled, but she didn't move.

"You think maybe... maybe you could—"

"I can shoot it. I can shoot it from right here." Sheila cut off Toby's words, her own voice a raspy whisper in the darkened shop.

"No!" Toby hissed his reply. "If CJ was telling any truth at all, I don't think that's a good idea."

The form outside swayed slightly from side to side, like a cobra studying its prey.

"How the hell did she... *it,* get out?" Sheila slowly moved from flat on her stomach to a sitting position, but the pistol never wavered from its aim.

Toby stepped gingerly over the stinking vinegar and spiced juices of the jarred meats toward Sheila. "I've got a feeling the hole wasn't sealed shut on purpose."

The broken window rattled and Toby froze in place. The shadow began to rock back and forth faster, as if it was agitated.

Or, excited, Toby thought, *like a cat watching canaries in a birdcage.*

"Sheila?"

"Yeah?"

"I want you to very slowly put the pistol on the floor."

"I ain't droppin' a bead on that fucked up thi—"

"Put the fucking gun on the floor!"

Sheila released a sigh of disgust, but Toby watched her ease the gun down to the tile. She crossed her arms and looked like a pouting toddler.

The swaying, excited movement slowed some, and then, as they all watched, the pair of crimson eyes moved toward the front door. A high keening mewl could be heard even though it was muffled by the barrier between them.

It was hunched down, moving on all fours, and Toby gritted his teeth as he watched the front door part ways from the doorframe so carefully the bell didn't even jingle.

"Ohhh fuck." Darlene whispered.

"Don't move." Toby motioned a hand to stop her, even though she was staring at the front door.

It moved inside the shop and froze in place, not even a flicker in those unblinking eyes.

Toby took a step forward. Then another. He put the toe of his right foot out toward the corpse and nudged it. It barely moved, but a fresh flow of blood escaped from beneath it. The shadow got the idea. It came further into the dark shop, stopped beside the corpse on the floor, and maneuvered down.

The sound of something wet and sloppy cut through the silence and Toby looked away toward the ceiling tiles. They all held their breath as the thing began to feed.

CHAPTER TWENTY-SEVEN

After being absolutely still and quiet for long minutes, it became apparent Abigail wasn't all that interested in the tired, frazzled people in the store. She lapped and gnawed and chewed and swallowed literal pounds of the dead Fake Fed and was now laying on her side, arching her back, stretched out and satisfied next to the corpse. Her small hands kneaded the torn flesh of the man's body. From her throat, a deep rumble emitted. She was *purring*. She rolled onto her side and curled her hands against Toby's shaking legs like a cat.

It made his skin crawl but he stood dead still.

"The fuck?" Toby whispered but masked it with a sigh, despite the feeling of wanting to jerk free and run from the store, anywhere at all to get the fuck away from this. He saw movement off to his left and noted CJ was stirring from his short bout with unconsciousness. He saw the man's bleary eyes flutter open, and quick as he could, Toby held a finger up to his mouth and shook his head side to side with an accentuation in the direction of the girl-thing and the half-eaten cadaver.

CJ's gaze floated in the girl's direction and he sat bolt upright, all color draining from his battered face. He looked to Sheila, hunkered beside the display of windshield washer fluid, her eyes wide and scared. He swung his gaze to Toby and then back to the monster now acting like a glutton-drunk cat.

"For fuck's sake... I forgot to lock the lid." CJ's

ROBERT FORD AND JOHN BODEN

gasping statement sounded rusty.

They both watched Abigail for any sign of acknowledgement. There were none, and shackled by their own fear, they all sat there and waited, for *what* they did not know. The purring faded and soon the air was filled with rhythmic snoring which seemed to sync to the hum of the fluorescent lights above them.

Their focus was so intent on the girl-thing that none of them noticed Darlene had somehow slipped from behind the counter and out the door, not even managing to make the bell above the door jingle in her absence.

Goddamn it, Toby thought. *Not like she was going to go to the cops, but she fucking left us. LEFT US!*

The girl-thing still had her limp hands curled around his ankles purring with satisfaction. Sleeping.

Toby considered taking a step back, easing himself away from her grip.

And then he saw the figure at the front door.

CHAPTER TWENTY-EIGHT

That fucking thing was unnatural.

Darlene opened the door to the dead Fed's truck. She knew the shotgun was there, behind the driver's seat, but there was no real reason to take it earlier.

Now, however... there most definitely was. What in the blue fuck *was* that thing? She'd listened to CJ blather for over an hour and he never did pin the fuckin' tail on this particular donkey. Whatever the fuck that thing was, it was gonna be dead in very short order.

She pulled the shotgun from the rack and shucked a shell in place. The noise was loud in the empty lot. Darlene stepped away from the truck and stood, bathed in moonlight, and stared at the husk of the dark store.

I could walk. Fuck, I could run from this place and never look back. I don't really know any of them except for that crazy bitch Sheila, and what real *loss would she be?*

Darlene had stepped free as the thing, *Abigail*, had begun eating from of the corpse. Watched as she tore a strip of flesh from the dead man's face, a peel of bloody tissue as thin and fragile as wrapping paper, and curled it on her tongue to pull it in her mouth.

Un-fucking-natural. And those eyes? What the fuck was up with those eyes? Kill it. Kill the goddamn thing dead. Deader than dogshit.

Darlene took a long breath, looking at the

almost-full moon overhead, sighed heavily and started walking briskly toward the store.

CHAPTER TWENTY-NINE

Toby glanced up from the pressure against his ankle. He was in the middle of easing away from Abigail's grip, his heart thumping against his rib cage, praying she wouldn't wake up in the process. The feel of the warm breath through the denim on his legs made his skin crawl.

A skinny shadow was at the front door and one he easily recognized—Darlene.

But, Darlene with something gripped in her hands.

The glass door opened slowly, carefully, and Darlene stepped inside. Just as carefully, she let the door shut behind her.

Why in the fuck does anyone have those bells on the door anyway? In a shop as small as this, does anyone really think they won't see and hear a customer coming in?

Toby held his breath and turned his gaze toward the sleeping *thing*. It didn't move in its slumber.

Darlene stepped closer and put the barrel of her shotgun inches away from the girl-thing's temple. She tilted her head one direction and then the other. Toby heard the gentle click of bones popping in her neck.

CJ inhaled sharply. Toby glanced at him to see him shaking his head.

"No. She's tied to me! No!" He hissed.

Darlene's face became a grimace. Toby watched as she stiffened her stance, hardened her pose and gripped the shotgun. He closed his eyes and waited for the blast.

Darlene's finger squeezed quickly.

CHAPTER THIRTY

The silence seemed to swell in the split second after she pulled the trigger. The unnatural quiet swirled and filled the store, as Darlene looked down at the sleeping creature, and then to the weapon in her shaking hands. She held it up close to her face and saw it was still ready to go, she pointed it at the thing once more and pulled the trigger. Nothing.

A small cough fluttered across the air.

They all looked at CJ, who was leaning against the shelves, his eyes bulging as he vehemently shook his head. Darlene frowned and looked down once more at the slumbering monster. She tilted the barrel downward and pulled the trigger again. There was no deafening blast—no cacophonous explosion to mark the discharge of the firearm— but CJ's head exploded just the same. It was an almost slow motion dismantling. The brain, and the skull that held it, reduced to shrapnel. Sheila screamed as her face and cleavage were splattered with gore and the ceiling was suddenly stuccoed in blood. Toby flinched from the spray of it all.

Darlene just stood there and looked at the dead man as his legs and arms spasmed, filthy work pants darkening with urine fleeing from his bladder. The shotgun fell from her hands to the floor and Darlene opened her mouth to scream at the Abigail-thing. It was staring her right in the eyes, with *those* fucking eyes, and smiling.

Then it blinked at her and Darlene fainted dead away.

Chapter Thirty-One

Toby stood stock still, until his legs went numb. The Abigail-thing purred in her renewed slumber. He eased one foot back, and then the other, fraction by fraction, until her small hands drifted free from his ankle. Her breathing hitched as she turned onto her side and he could see the blood, dried where it had soaked her face. Her purring commenced.

The corpse on the floor had his throat torn apart. The edges of the wound at his Adam's Apple glistened in the dim light. Toby couldn't break his gaze.

Was this how the children had died? How his little sister had died?

He wanted to stomp the thing… stomp its head and cave it in until it was nothing but a smear on the dirty floor like CJ's brains. Hot rage flooded through him.

"I'm um…" Sheila stood up in the puddle of CJ's remains. Her arms were in front of her, hands clasped together like a little kid. "I'm just…" She started walking, on her tiptoes like a child, and made her way around the dead Fed, leaving bloody footprints from her sneakers.

"Sheila?" Toby's whisper was laden with panic and anxiety.

She paused by Darlene's prone body, but she never even glanced at the girl on the floor. Sheila turned to Toby and he saw a silver thread of drool from her lips. She gave him the gentlest smile and shook her head slightly, as if trying to dismiss the world she lived in right now.

"I think I'm just... I wanna go home." She swung the door open, making the bells jingle, and put a hand against her bloody face. *"Shhhh."*

Toby stood alone.

CHAPTER THIRTY-TWO

Sheila pulled her car keys from her jean pocket and floated toward her car. That's how she felt, at least—floating. Everything looked flickery, like there was one of those Halloween strobe lights in her head. She wrapped her arms around herself.

Cold. It's so... cold. Why is it so cold?

The keys jangled as she shivered. She opened her car door and slid into the driver's seat. Sheila started the engine and flipped the heater on full blast. She looked into her rearview mirror and nodded to herself, and then threw the car in reverse and backed it up close to the gas pumps.

Still shivering, Sheila got out of the car and pulled a gas nozzle free of its holster.

"Fire is the Devil's only friend." She sang as she stuck the nozzle in the open back window of the vehicle and squeezed the trigger.

CATTYWAMPUS

CHAPTER THIRTY-THREE

"Darlene!" Toby whispered as loud as he dared, but there was no movement from the girl. He stepped into Sheila's bloody footprints and made his way across the store. The dark outline of the shotgun was in his periphery and he wanted to grab it, rack a shell and unload it into the thing sleeping behind him.

But what the hell had happened when Darlene tried to blast her? What is *she?*

He recalled CJ's remark about it—*her*—being tied to him now. It reminded him of a poem he'd liked in high school about a dude on a ship that had accidentally killed an albatross and, in doing that, had condemned his ship and crew to damnation.

Toby crouched by Darlene and shook her shoulder, whispering again. "Hey, Darlene! Wake up." He brushed his hand across her face. "Darlene!"

In the low light, her face looked placid. Peaceful. Beautiful.

He shook her harder and her eyes flickered, focusing on the ceiling, and then Toby's face.

The light shining on her grew brighter—much brighter than it should be—and Toby heard the screaming engine of a car bearing down on the front of the store.

CHAPTER THIRTY-FOUR

Sheila slammed on the brakes and the tires squealed to a stop less than six yards from the doors. She saw Toby and Darlene bathed in the muted light from the filthy headlights. She sat in the driver's seat and shook. Her goose-pimpled flesh was moon pale. The smell of the gasoline fumes from the soaked rear seat swirled around her like petroleum ghosts. She held her foot on the brake and watched Toby slide his arms under Darlene's shoulders. Sheila frowned as she watched him clasp his hands beneath Darlene's breasts.

Sheila felt the tears begin to threaten as she found herself mumbling a litany of petty jealous vitriol more befitting to a ninth grader than a forty-something skank. She tilted her head and watched Toby get the younger girl upright, he slung an arm around her waist and they slowly walked toward the door.

He doesn't want a thing to do with a crusty old gash like you.

Sheila turned to the back seat, trying to find the source of the voice. All that resided back there was a pile of old dirty shirts and hoodies and a pair old cowboy boots. All sopping with fuel. She looked back to the store and saw the couple was nearly to the door. Sheila eased her foot off the brake, ready to get going the moment they were in line.

He thinks you're disgusting, babe. Wouldn't give you a drillin' if you was the last oil field in Texas, sweetheart. Fat. Old. Slut.

"Shut up!" Sheila barked to no one in the vehicle. She saw her teeth bared in the rearview mirror, glanced down, and saw Toby with his hand on the door handle. He was smiling. It was a sideways smirk full of condemnation and tepid pity.

You couldn't even wrangle a pity fuck outta that boy. He wants to get deep in Darlene... he wouldn't thumbfuck you during a blackout, you cow!

The tears flowed freely now. She knew the voice was right. It always was. She sniffled back the salty snot into her mouth and spat it on the floor. She looked up and saw Toby and Darlene pushing the door open slowly. She saw his left hand clutching Darlene's side under her tit and his right hand on her hip to steady her. He looked up at Sheila and smiled, his tongue poking out, wetting his thin lips slowly.

Wouldn't piss on you if you was on fire, girl.

Sheila dropped her foot on the gas pedal like it was a bundle of bricks. Tires squealed in the night.

The car lurched forward.

CHAPTER THIRTY-FIVE

Toby screamed and lunged to his right, pulling Darlene with him.

Sheila roared by, missing them by inches.

Toby's first thought as they slammed to the cement and road flare agony erupted in his arm was *My fuckin' elbow. I broke my elbow. But I saved the girl.* They landed in front of the tall, bagged ice cooler as shattering glass filled the air behind them.

Toby reflexively shut his eyes as the chips rained down on his face and over his body. There was the terrible noise of rending metal and destruction. The stink of gasoline was thick in the air, and the softest noise— a gentle whimper and sound of crying, from Sheila in the driver's seat.

Toby heard a low *whump* noise from inside the store right as he registered the smell of natural gas.

CHAPTER THIRTY-SIX

A massive fireball detonated the indigo night of Steelwater. The front windows of the store blew out in a rainstorm of glass. Something heavy and metallic crashed against the pavement like a B52. Toby felt the explosion swarm around him and pain, bright and pristine in its agony, kissed the flesh of his exposed cheekbone and engulfed his arm. The pain hit a crescendo and then gave way to a static buzzing in its numbness.

Toby screamed and rolled to his side, covering his burning arm with his body. The entire world was smoke and flame and falling debris. He grabbed Darlene's hand and struggled to his knees to help her up. Wisps of smoke drifted from strands of the girl's hair and she focused on Toby with dazed, terrified eyes. Chunks of burning wood and shingles littered the lot. Flames reached through the shattered storefront, surrounding Sheila's fuel-soaked car halfway through the entrance. Fire covered the hood and through the busted windshield. Toby turned away from the silhouette in the car flames.

"Come on!" He yanked Darlene to her feet, and half-dragged, half-walked her in the direction of the road. The cooler chest of bagged ice that had sat beside the front door was now a twisted mass of scorched metal near the gas pumps. A single cooler door held on by one warped hinge, but the other door had been torn free. A trail of ice and burning plastic bags revealed the cooler's journey.

A sharp snapping noise came from behind and then another explosion as Sheila's car erupted. The blast knocked Toby to his knees and Darlene fell with him. More debris fell from the sky.

Toby helped Darlene to her feet again and made it the edge of the lot. They both fell to the thick patch of grass. "Are you…" Toby broke into a coughing fit and he doubled over, turning his face toward the road and away from the smoke. He wheezed, drawing in a breath, and then turned toward Darlene. "Are you okay?"

The girl's expression was vacant, her connection to reality tenuous. Darlene slowly turned her head and reached her right arm out to Toby. She paused and Toby followed her gaze.

The flesh of the girl's forearm was blackened into a crust, cracked and open to reveal pink tissue beneath. Darlene released a sharp laugh. Her eyes drifted back to Toby. "We made it." She whispered.

"Looks like it." Toby looked at her reddened face, the twists and knots of melted strands of hair. He knew he had shielded Darlene as much as he could, but if she looked this bad, he wasn't anxious to find a mirror anytime soon. Patches of his skin almost felt cold and he knew damned well that couldn't be a good sign.

Darlene nestled against him and closed her eyes.

Toby just kept watching the fire and the face he imagined he saw in it.

CHAPTER THIRTY-SEVEN

The Steelwater fire crew frantically sprayed the store until water flooded from the building onto the asphalt around it. And still, there were blossoms of fire reigniting. There were screams about cutting off the gas line but Toby could barely make out the words. His head thrummed, hearing dulled, and he could feel his heartbeat inside his skull.

Cops arrived on the heels of the fire crew and started asking questions. Toby nodded at the officers and provided vague answers. After a while, they left him alone and the medics worked on Toby's face and arm as the cops put their attention on Darlene. The girl still appeared disconnected from the world around her, and Toby wondered if she had gotten a concussion of if it was the events of the night.

A medic had wrapped a blanket around Toby and he pulled it tighter, shivering, as he watched the medic attend to the burns on his arm.

"You're lucky to be alive, kid." The medic looked up at Toby's face and winced. "We ain't never seen shit like this."

"Do I need to go to the hospital?"

"Well…" The medic reached a gloved hand toward his face, lightly touching Toby's chin to gently move his head. "You probably should just to get checked out, but as for your burns," the man chewed his lip and glanced behind him. He lowered his voice. "I'm guessin' you don't have insurance?"

Toby shook his head and the medic nodded.

"Look, man. Your arm is one thing. Your hoodie

has seen better days and I peeled away the melted shit from your skin. Keep putting burn ointment on it and keep it clean." The man's eyes leveled at Toby, emphasizing his point. "Clean, you hear me?"

"Got it."

"Your arm will be okay. Your face, though."

He prodded at the skin and Toby gritted his teeth. The pain and sensation was back.

"You've got some blistered skin but no third degree. How the hell you managed that is…" The medic shook his head. "You'll probably have some scarring, but same thing as your arm. Keep it clean. Keep ointment on it and in between reapplying, it's not a—" he glanced around again to see if other medics were close by. "Mix up some sugar paste and put it on there for a couple hours. Or honey. Whatever you got."

Toby was too tired to bother asking questions, but the man's advice didn't sound official.

"It'll fix you up."

Toby looked at Darlene. Another medic was wiping smudges from her pretty face. "And her?"

"That arm of hers is in bad shape. She's headed to the Burn Unit."

***

They loaded Darlene into the back of the ambulance and drove off. A few pick-ups tried to stop along the road to watch the drama and an officer had waved them off.

Toby sat and watched as another firetruck

from Thurmont rolled into the lot and an additional crew joined in to get things under control. The parking lot was a soup of ashen water that stank of staunched embers. The building was a pile of smoldering cinders and blackened girders sticking from the rubble like rotted fingers. Toby sat in the weeds and watched as they withdrew Sheila's body from her car. Most of the remaining meat slid from her bones like all-day roasted BBQ ribs. The char on her body shimmered in the light like black diamonds. Two firemen stumbled away from the car and ripped their facemasks free.

"Christ!" One of the officers dry-heaved and spun away from the scene, sputtering and shaking his head. "Jesus Christ." He stopped and put his hands on his knees, dry-heaving and spitting. He looked up at Toby. "Kid. I'll drive you wherever you want to go, but you can't stay here anymore."

Toby stood on weak legs and followed the officer to his patrol car.

He told him where to drive and a mile from the scene, the patrol radio crackled.

"Noble?"

The cop reached for the radio. "Noble here. Go."

"You're gonna…" Static popped and the line went silent, then came on again. "You're gonna want to come back to the scene."

The officer sighed through gritted teeth. "I'm driving a bystander home right now. What's up?"

There was a pause on the line, and then "Noble, we got inside and there's bodies there. Nothin' goddamned left of them but meat and shattered—"

"I said I've got a bystander in the car with me, right now."

Toby saw the cop glance at him and then click the radio again. "Coroner's on his way so—"

"Sir, it's not the bodies. We found a bucket in the store cooler. It's melted but there's… Noble, there's human teeth in it. A lot of them."

Toby turned to stare out the window, ignoring the rest of what the cop said as he drove onward.

Chapter Thirty-Seven

Toby woke up in his own bed, lying on top of the covers. He didn't remember laying down or falling asleep, but here he was, still wearing the clothes he was driven home in. His hoodie was stained with blood and smelled of smoke and spent fuel. He turned over onto his side and stared at the open door to the hallway. He sighed and willed himself into a sitting position, though his muscles and bones ached with the effort. A scalding hot shower and then a visit to the hospital to see Darlene seemed the right things to do. He rose and shuffled to the bathroom.

"Weirdest fucking day, ever." Toby mumbled and pulled the sweatshirt over his head. He almost dropped it on the floor, but tossed it into the open trash bin by the sink instead. He wanted a shower to wash off as much of the night as possible, but he knew the memory itself would stay embedded in his mind.

Were the water not rushing over his ears, Toby would have heard the screech of the spring on the screen door as it opened, and the sound of soft footsteps in the hall.

CHAPTER THIRTY-EIGHT

A burned to the ground gas station isn't high on the list of sought-after properties in a town like Steelwater. The charred remains sat vacant and mostly ignored while people in town shifted and adapted and bought their six-packs of Bud and cancer sticks in town and pumped their gas at the QwikMart on the East End.

Time moved on, slow and steady, like the brackish waters of the Steelwater River.

As Toby had predicted, the police had more questions. He volunteered to go down to the station to talk instead of having them come by the house.

It made things less complicated.

Four bodies were found among the ashes of the station. Toby gave answers about one of them without mentioning her by name.

I stopped in to grab a cold drink and I didn't even make it inside the place. Next thing I know, that girl came haulin' ass like Fast and the Furious right into the shop. I barely got out of there alive. Don't know nothin' about the other bodies.

They stared and they glared, but Toby had no prior record—not even so much as a speeding ticket—and since the cameras hadn't been recording anything at the gas station, there was no reason to hold him.

Toby had never made it to see Darlene in the hospital, though a week later, she stopped by his house and knocked at the locked door. He kept quiet inside and watched her shadow through the living room curtains until she got back in her car and drove away.

He liked Darlene well enough, and was impressed with the way she had handled herself through everything even more. Toby wished he could have seen her, let her in, speak in person about everything.

But it was better this way.

No... Toby thought. *It* had *to be this way.*

Abigail was getting hungry.

An' if'n you keep her fed, she's a sweet little thing.

He stood on the front stoop and balanced the large bag of McDonald's on his injured arm and thumbed the key into the door lock of his double-wide. Toby heard movement on the other side of the door and drew a deep breath before pushing it open.

Three months rolled by before another child went missing in Steelwater.

The End

Robert Ford has written the novels *The Compound*, and *No Lipstick in Avalon*, the novellas *Ring of Fire, The Last Firefly of Summer, Samson and Denial,* and *Bordertown,* as well as the short story collection *The God Beneath my Garden.*

He has co-authored the novella *Rattlesnake Kisses* with John Boden, and the novel *A Penny For Your Thoughts* with Matt Hayward.

In addition, he has several screenplays floating around in the ether of Hollywood.

He can confirm the grass actually is greener on the other side, but it's only because of the bodies buried there.

You can find out more about what he's up to by visiting robertfordauthor.com

*Photo by Becky Brown
of Brown Photography*

John Boden lives a stones throw from Three Mile Island with his wonderful wife and sons. A baker by day, he spends his off time writing or watching old television shows. He likes Diet Pepsi and sports ferocious sideburns. He loves heavy metal and old country music. And shoofly pie. He's a pretty nice fella, honest.

His work has appeared in *Borderlands 6, Shock Totem, Splatterpunk, Lamplight, Blight Digest*, the John Skipp edited *Psychos* and others. His not-really-for-children children's book, *Dominoes* has been called a pretty cool thing. His other books, *Jedi Summer With the Magnetic Kid* and *Detritus In Love* are out and about. He recently released a novella with fellow author Chad Lutzke called *Out Behind the Barn*.

He has a slew of things on the horizon.

60843847R00066

Made in the USA
Middletown, DE
17 August 2019